DUNGEONS & DRAGONS

THE MINI BAG OF HOLDING INVENTORY BOOK

T0364067

RP Minis®
Hachette Book Group
1290 Avenue of the Americas, New York, NY 10104
www.runningpress.com
@Running_Press

First Edition: September 2021

Published by RP Minis, an imprint of Perseus Books, LLC, a subsidiary of Hachette Book Group, Inc. The RP Minis name and logo is a registered trademark of the Hachette Book Group.

The Hachette Speakers Bureau provides a wide range of authors for speaking events. To find out more, go to www.hachettespeakersbureau.com or call (866) 376-6591.

The publisher is not responsible for websites (or their content) that are not owned by the publisher.

ISBN: 978-0-7624-7590-2

IF YOU'RE READING THIS, then I've got myself a problem. Because if you're reading this, then that means that my most precious possession has slipped from my person and found its way into yours. While this bag may look like your typical satchel, I can assure you, it's just as mysterious as the smile etched across its front.

This book serves as a log, an inventory of items that I have procured through roundabout or unwholesome ways. Some things I came across on my own but, in my line of work, lifting items from the unsuspecting and doubling their worth is all part of the job. However, some things are too precious to sell to just *anyone*, and many of the objects within this bag are more valuable to me than a king's ransom. You might find it strange for someone of my nature to keep a record, but the bag itself has many secrets and it would not surprise me to come across an item or two that I don't recall *collecting*.

Perhaps fortune will guide this bag back into my possession, but until then, finders, keepers.

ITEM 001—CLEANSING STONE

When I was young, I lived in a quiet provincial town. I was often left to my own devices and, as a result, was repeatedly scolded by my mother for dirtying up my freshly cleaned boots and jerkins. One afternoon, while wandering around the forest, I came across a rock with strange markings carved into it. I shoved the stone into my boot and hurried home, noticing once again, that my boots were caked with globs of mud and leaves. At the threshold, I desperately wished my mother wouldn't notice . . . but as I tried to scrape off what I could, I realized that my boots were suddenly clean. At the time, I wasn't sure how this had happened, but I would later learn that the stone had cleansing properties. This unique stone has aided in pulling off my dirtiest jobs ever since.

Item 002- Scimitar

I make it a point to avoid melee scuffles at all costs, but there are times when I'll admit that buttered words will do no good against brutish hostility. I found this particular blade plunged deep into a sack of grain while traveling aboard a ship full of sketchy tradesmen. While this weapon isn't particularly my style, it does have a great story. During our voyage, the captain would challenge his crew to a ritual-like game of chance whenever we anchored at port.

The only problem was that the captain would always win. Noticing my own kind is second nature and, while I'm all for a clever con or some simple trickery, I didn't care for the captain or his boasting. It was all too easy to hint to his first mate that perhaps the captain's run of luck was a little *too* fortuitous. When the captain lost that night, accusations were made, and the first mate only managed to keep his head due to the many flagons of rum the captain consumed. Chaos broke out on the ship after that, so I took up the scimitar for protection, relieved a few unconscious pirates of their valuables—which included the captain's pair of enchanted dice—and promptly made my escape.

ITEM 003—WAND OF CONDUCTING

I picked up this wand from the belt of an old bard who frequented a tavern I used to pass through up north. He often used it to enhance his performance of epic ballads, producing symphonic accompaniments, while he yammered on about a strapping young hero or band of protectors slaying dragons or exposing corrupt kings. Of course, I meant to sell it, but over the years, I've come to understand now how useful a melody can be—especially as a delightful distraction at a sophisticated event where you're trying to loot gold from an old nobleman's treasure troves.

ITEM 004- DISGUISE SELF SPELL

This item was payment for stealing a chest full of diamonds for an old wizard. He assured me that I would not be disappointed as he pressed it into my hand before he departed. At first, I didn't realize what it was for, but when I started to read the scroll aloud, I immediately stopped when I realized that it was a *spell* scroll allowing me to disguise my visage for a short period of time—but it can be used only once! I'm keeping it handy for when I'm faced with an extremely challenging heist.

ITEM 005 · SPYGLASS

I picked this off a petite pirate at the port in Waterdeep. It was a rather damp, dreary night, but she must have had a good time because she was stumbling back to her "trade ship" with a few of her equally drunk compatriots. I was walking a few paces behind in poor spirits because I had spent most of the night staking out a rather boring noble's house, when the woman tripped on a loose plank at the docks. Her companions must not have realized that she had fallen, which spared her dignity, I guess, so I helped her up. I was expecting a rough comment or gruff response, but because of her soft embarrassed smile and genuine thanks, I only took her looking glass. I often use it to study those who I'm looking to steal from and I often find myself reminiscing about her when I do.

ITEM 006—MECHANICAL SPIDER

This little fella is my most favored trick and means of distraction—the mechanical arachnid. I had him made by a dwarven engineer a few years back for a special job. He will move about when no one is looking; however, he will stop any time someone sets eyes on him. In between big jobs, he is great for entertaining folks while I pick a few pockets and bags for potions and a few pieces of silver. Don't even get me started about those who are afraid of spiders—because then I almost feel bad for stealing from

them—but hey, it works like a charm
every time, so can you blame me?

ITEM 007- ALCHEMY JUG

This item is a *souvenir* of probably one of the most trying quests I've been on to date. I took this jug from the corner of a shrine for the followers of a man carrying a crocodile on his back. I don't quite remember the reason why I took this particular object or if there were other—possibly more valuable treasures around—but luck was on my side because at least it was useful.

The jug produced its own water, which kept me nice and hydrated, especially fortuitous after losing one of my water-skins to the jungle's depths. Luckily, and to my complete surprise, it also held the capability to make beer as well . . . which helped me maintain the remaining scraps of my sanity for the month-long journey with a pompous and finicky high elf.

ITEM 008—CAPE OF THE MOUNTEBANK

I swiped this suspicious item from a wizard who had hired me for a simple, albeit boring job—deliver the cape to a sorcerer in the next town over. Though I thought the task beneath me, I intended to complete it because I was low on funds. I should have suspected that the cape wouldn't be ordinary given that it belonged to someone training in arcane magic, but at the time, the only thing on my mind was the weight of a few extra coins in my pocket at the end of the task—that and whether the cape would suit my tastes. I threw it over my shoulders to see and was instantly teleported out of the wizard's citadel. In fact, when my wits finally returned, I realized that I was now all the way across town by the docks. I've been holding onto this cape for many years now.

ITEM 009—BOOK OF EXALTED DEEDS

A few months back, I stole this tome from a paladin that had joined my party for a short time during our travels. He carried on and on about wanting to bring great fortune to his god's devoted servants and every night would sit up reading this book. Since acquiring it,

I've heard rumors say the tome will go from person to person, enriching their lives once it's read, but only if they're of good will. The paladin wasn't quite finished reading it when I plucked it from his bag before we parted ways. The whole concept is a little too righteous for me, so I've decided to leave it here until the right buyer comes along.

ITEM 010—GOLDFISH IN AN ORB

This is Henry, my goldfish and favorite travel companion. A few years back, while on a job for a drow, I found him swimming alone in a large fountain in an unsavory part of town. Since the fountain was off the beaten path, I wasn't expecting to find anything more than some stagnant water and maybe a copper or two for my troubles. Instead, I found him swimming in the lower tier. When I saw his adorable listless eyes, I knew I had to keep him! I secured him in an old potion orb I'd received in my share of treasure from a recent adventure, and we've been together ever since. He's a good listener and my favorite color.

ITEM 011—RING OF X-RAY VISION

It isn't rare for me to spot other thieves and con artists; however, it's difficult to find those that I'm willing to work or travel with. That said, I once found myself in the company of a band of halflings who happened to share the same enthusiasm for procuring unique and unusual items that didn't belong to us. While together, I learned many tricks and was thoroughly impressed with their ability to pinpoint treasures on the job with great ease. Then, one night after a few celebratory drinks, I learned the key to their success——they had a ring that allowed them to see through solid objects!

Of course, now that I knew their secret, I had to take it for myself. So, when they were bickering later over who would wear it for the next job, I told them I would hold onto it until the dispute was settled. I still can't believe or understand why they trusted me, but they did. As soon as the ring was in my hand, I quickly threw on my teleportation cape and never looked back.

ITEM 012—TRIDENT OF FISH COMMAND

At the bottom of a murky lake in Neverwinter there was rumored to be a lost chest of jewels, which is, incidentally, where I also happened to find this trident. After many hours of searching, I finally located the chest only to find that there was nothing inside of it. Nearby, half-buried in the silty lake bottom, I noticed this curious trident. Not wishing to go home empty-handed, I grabbed it and started to make my way to the surface. It was then that I noticed something strange—I was able to understand and communicate with the lake's fishy inhabitants with my mind! This was quite a turn in my fortune. After persuading my newfound friends with some sob story, they led me to the real sunken treasure, which had been buried in the remains of a sunken dinghy.

ADDITIONAL ARTIST CREDITS

Christopher Burdett, Conceptopolis, Cory Trego-Erdner, Irina Nordsol, Joel Thomas, Lake Hurwitz, Wayne England

This book has been bound using
handcraft methods and Smyth-sewn
to ensure durability.

The package and interior were
designed by Rachel Peckman

The text was written
by Brenna Dinon